Barkley

REBECCA CRANE

WALKER BOOKS
AND SUBSIDIARIES

LONDON • BOSTON • SYDNEY • AUCKLAND

For my mum and dad
– RC

First published 2020 by Walker Books Ltd
87 Vauxhall Walk, London SE11 5HJ

2 4 6 8 10 9 7 5 3 1

This book has been typeset in
ITC Mendoza Roman and Hunterswood

Printed in China

British Library Cataloguing in Publication Data: a catalogue
record for this book is available from the British Library

ISBN 978-1-4063-9598-3

www.walker.co.uk

My name is Barkley!
I'm a dog.

I'm a very **BIG** dog!

OK, I'm not a very big dog.

I'm a **fluffy** dog!

Not THAT fluffy.

I'm a **loooooooong** dog!

Oh. No, I'm not.

I'm a ~~FANCY~~ dog.

I'm a ~~FIERCE~~ dog.

I'm a ~~FAST~~ dog.

WHAT KIND OF
DOG AM I?

Maybe I'm just a **NOTHING** dog.

WAIT!
BARKLEY,
COME BACK!

Wait a minute.
Where's Max?

Where am I?

I'm a very, very lost dog.

Look! That's me!

LOST

A SMALL BLACK AND WHITE DOG. HE IS MY BEST FRIEND. PLEASE COME HOME BARKLEY!

I must find Max!

Have you seen my friend?

Now I know exactly
what kind of dog I am.

I'm a **small** dog,

and a **black and white** dog,

and a **BEST FRIEND** kind of dog!

Which makes me ...

a very, very **HAPPY** dog!